Piggy Party

Beverly Lewis

Beverly Lewis Books for Young Readers

PICTURE BOOK

Cows in the House

THE CUL-DE-SAC KIDS

The Double Dabble Surprise
The Chicken Pox Panic
The Crazy Christmas Angel Mystery
No Grown-ups Allowed
Frog Power
The Mystery of Case D. Luc
The Stinky Sneakers Mystery
Pickle Pizza
Mailbox Mania
The Mudhole Mystery
Fiddlesticks
The Crabby Cat Caper
Tarantula Toes
Green Gravy
Backyard Bandit Mystery
Tree House Trouble
The Creepy Sleep-Over
The Great TV Turn-Off
Piggy Party
The Granny Game

The Six-Hour Mystery
Mystery at Midnight
Katie and Jake and the Haircut Mistake

THE CUL-DE-SAC KIDS

Piggy Party

Beverly Lewis

BETHANY HOUSE PUBLISHERS
MINNEAPOLIS, MINNESOTA 55438

Published by Bethany House Publishers
A Ministry of Bethany Fellowship International
11400 Hampshire Avenue South
Minneapolis, Minnesota 55438
www.bethanyhouse.com

Printed in the United States of America by
Bethany Press International, Minneapolis, Minnesota 55438
ISBN 0–7642–2124–8

To
Talon Zachary Erickson,
my new friend in Minnesota.

THE CUL-DE-SAC KIDS

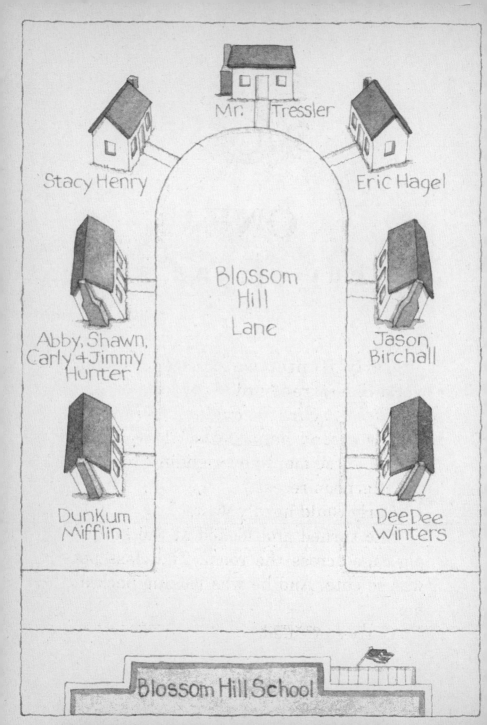

Mr. Tressler

Stacy Henry

Eric Hagel

Blossom
Hill
Lane

Abby, Shawn,
Carly & Jimmy
Hunter

Jason
Birchall

Dunkum
Mifflin

DeeDee
Winters

Blossom Hill School

ONE

Carly Hunter watched the school clock. She stared hard.

Click . . . click . . . click.

The second hand poked along like a turtle. Three more never-ending minutes till afternoon recess.

Carly could hardly wait.

She turned and looked at the guinea pig cage across the room. The class pet was so cute. And he was looking back at her!

Carly squirmed.

She jiggled.

Her school desk danced, too.

Dee Dee Winters tapped Carly on the shoulder. "You're a wiggle worm today," she whispered.

Dee Dee was Carly's best friend. She sat right behind Carly at school. The perfect spot for a best friend.

Carly said softly, "I have the flitter-flops."

"You're not kidding," said Dee Dee.

Carly was still watching the furry pet. "I can't believe I get to take the guinea pig home. All weekend."

"His name is Piggy, don't forget," Dee Dee reminded her.

Carly grinned. "Who could forget a name like that?"

Dee Dee smiled and twisted a curl.

"Girls, please get busy," said Miss Hartman. The teacher's voice was kind but firm.

Carly picked up her pencil. She printed her name neatly. She tried to do her workbook pages. But her eyes wanted to wander to Piggy's cage!

"Miss Hartman's watching you," she heard Dee Dee whisper.

Quickly, Carly looked down at her work sheet. She would have to cover up her head. She just couldn't keep her eyes off the guinea pig.

Carly glanced at the clock above the door again.

Goody!

The recess bell would be ringing. Right . . . about . . . now.

BRRING!

"I call the swings," said one of the girls. She flew past Carly and Dee Dee.

Carly didn't care about swinging. Not today. She had more important things in mind. Things like feeding the guinea pig. Things like changing his water dish.

She hurried to Piggy's cage.

Dee Dee came, too. "Where are you gonna put Piggy at your house?" asked Dee Dee.

"I might hide him in the secret place, behind my closet," Carly said.

Dee Dee's eyes grew round as silver dollars. "He might not like it in there. It's too dark."

"But he'll be safe," Carly insisted. "Especially from my little brother."

"Why? What's Jimmy gonna do to Piggy?" Dee Dee asked.

"Nothing, if I keep Piggy hidden." Carly reached down into the cage. She removed the dish of water. She carried the dish to the sink and poured some fresh water.

Dee Dee leaned over the cage. "He's so soft and pretty."

"Looks like butterscotch," said Carly.

"Yummy," said Dee Dee.

Carly poked her friend. "Silly! Guinea pigs aren't candy."

Dee Dee shrugged. "But Piggy *is* the coolest class pet we've had all year."

Carly agreed. They'd had two lizards and even a garter snake before Christmas. But Piggy was the perfect class pet. He was easy to care for. He made the cutest sounds, too. Sometimes it sounded like he was whistling.

Carly liked that. Maybe she and Piggy would have a whistle duet this weekend. Maybe she and the guinea pig would celebrate Groundhog Day together.

Tomorrow!

She wondered if Piggy might see his shadow. After all, guinea pigs were related to groundhogs. Weren't they?

TWO

Carly and Dee Dee marched home through the snow. Carly pulled her sled with the guinea pig cage tied onto it. "I hope Piggy doesn't catch a cold," she said.

The girls stopped to check on the pet. They lifted the blanket off his cage.

"Aw, look, he's shivering," Carly said. She wished she'd asked her mother to pick her up at school. "We better hurry."

"He needs a little sweater," Dee Dee suggested.

"Whoever heard of a guinea pig wearing a sweater?" Carly said.

"We should make him one this weekend," Dee Dee said.

"Maybe," Carly said. She was more concerned about getting Piggy inside her warm house.

The girls lived on Blossom Hill Lane, right across from Blossom Hill School. There were seven houses and nine kids on the cul-de-sac. All nine kids were good friends. They even had a club and a favorite motto. Carly's big sister, Abby, was the president of the Cul-de-sac Kids.

"Are you gonna bring Piggy to the club meeting tonight?" Dee Dee asked.

Carly really didn't want to share Piggy with the Cul-de-sac Kids. He was *her* pet for the weekend! "Why should I bring Piggy?" Carly shot back.

"Well, why not?" Dee Dee said. "Pretend it's show-and-tell—like at school."

Carly shook her head. "That's silly."

Dee Dee wrinkled her nose.

Carly pulled the sled faster. She looked at the sky. "I wonder if the sun will shine tomorrow."

"The sun's *always* shining," Dee Dee said. "We learned that in science, remember? You just can't always see the sun."

"Because of the clouds," Carly said. She knew all that. "I'm not thinking about sunshine right now. I'm thinking about a famous groundhog."

Dee Dee clapped her mittened hands. "Because it's gonna be Groundhog Day soon."

"Right," said Carly. "What do you think about that groundhog in Pennsylvania? *He's* the one who sees his shadow every year," Carly said.

Dee Dee raised her eyebrows. "It

doesn't make sense, does it?"

Carly agreed. "An old groundhog crawls out of his hole and sees his shadow. So what! Is it *really* a sign that we're stuck with six more weeks of winter?"

"It oughta be the other way around," Dee Dee said. "If the sun's shining when the groundhog comes out, that means it's the *end* of winter. Right?"

"Yep. The whole thing is mixed up," Carly said.

She thought of the cute guinea pig.

Maybe Piggy would know if their long, snowy winter was almost over. Maybe he'd know something about the secret of the groundhog. And the shadow.

Maybe. . . .

THREE

Carly and Dee Dee carried the guinea pig cage inside.

"I have an idea," Carly told Dee Dee.

"What is it?" Dee Dee asked.

"Wait and see," said Carly. They hurried down the hallway to Carly's bedroom.

"Aw, please?" Dee Dee pleaded. "We're best friends, aren't we?" She'd used that line to hear secrets before.

Carly didn't say a word.

"When's the secret gonna happen?" asked Dee Dee.

"Tomorrow at high noon," Carly said. There was a ring of mystery in her voice.

Dee Dee sat on the edge of Carly's bed. "Is this about Groundhog Day?" she asked.

Carly felt like being a little tricky. "I'm going to find out if spring is coming soon."

Dee Dee's eyes grew wide again. "How?"

"Just show up here tomorrow. Twelve o'clock sharp." Carly went to the window and pulled back the curtains. She searched the sky. Heavy snow clouds hung low.

Dee Dee came over and stood by the window. "Carly Hunter, you're up to something. I just know it!"

Carly knew Dee Dee couldn't keep a secret. It was almost impossible!

"You can tell me," Dee Dee said. Her big brown eyes were ready to pop.

"No way," Carly said, laughing. She went to the cage and saw that Piggy had stopped shaking. "Look, he's warming up."

Dee Dee was begging. "C'mon, Carly! Don't change the subject. Tell me what's gonna happen tomorrow!"

"I won't spoil the surprise," Carly said. "It's a Groundhog Day secret." And she made her voice sound extra sneaky.

"Ple-e-ease?" Dee Dee begged.

Carly knelt beside the guinea pig cage. She didn't want to be mean. Or make Dee Dee mad at her. She wanted to have fun on Groundhog Day. She was tired of all the cold and snow. Carly had to find out if winter was nearly over.

But Dee Dee was still pleading. "I'll do anything you say, if you just tell me."

"Okay, okay," Carly finally gave in.

Dee Dee danced around the room. "Hoo-ray!"

"You *have* to keep it a secret," Carly said.

"I can do that," Dee Dee replied.

Carly really hoped so.

FOUR

Carly sat beside Dee Dee on the floor.

Time for the Cul-de-sac Kids club meeting. They usually met at Dunkum's house. He had the biggest basement. And his parents didn't mind.

Dunkum's real name was Edward, but everyone called him Dunkum. He could slam-dunk most any basketball. He was that tall!

The Cul-de-sac Kids always took off

their shoes before a meeting. They lined them up in a row.

Carly stared at the neat row of snow boots. She could hardly wait to wear tennis shoes again. And sandals and shorts. And go swimming with the warm sun shining down. . . .

"The meeting will come to order," Abby said. She was sitting in the giant beanbag. It was the president's chair.

"Where's Piggy?" Dee Dee whispered to Carly.

Carly said, "I left him at home. He's hiding."

Dee Dee had a crooked smile. "Did you hide him in the you-know-what place?"

Carly said, "Maybe I did, maybe I didn't."

Dee Dee twisted her short, wavy hair. "Don't be so snooty."

"Listen to the president," Carly replied. "Abby's talking."

"You better tell me," Dee Dee whispered.

"I don't have to," Carly said back.

Abby was shaking her head. "Excuse me, girls. We're trying to have a meeting here."

Dunkum Mifflin wagged his finger at Carly and Dee Dee. "Nobody talks when the president is talking."

Eric Hagel turned around and stared. His eyes weren't blinking at all.

"It's not nice to stare, Eric," Dee Dee hissed.

Carly poked Dee Dee in the ribs. "Be quiet!"

"I don't feel like it!" Dee Dee hollered.

Jason Birchall made a face at Carly and Dee Dee. "You two better watch it," he said.

Stacy Henry put her hands over her ears.

Shawn and Jimmy frowned at Carly and Dee Dee. Then they chattered to each other in Korean.

Dee Dee stood up. She looked down at Carly. Then she twirled a curl with her finger.

Carly wondered what Dee Dee was up to. She felt jittery.

Dee Dee raised her hand to speak.

"Yes, Dee Dee?" Abby said from the front of the room.

"Carly's hiding a guinea pig in her closet," Dee Dee blurted. "She doesn't want anyone to know."

How could she do this to me? Carly wondered.

"It's true, just ask her," Dee Dee was saying.

"It's NOT true!" Carly yelled back. She wasn't lying. She was hiding Piggy *behind* the closet wall.

Abby jumped out of her beanbag. "I think we'd better call this meeting quits," she said.

Dee Dee sat right down. "We'll be quiet. We promise."

Abby nodded her head. "It's been a long and cold winter. Everyone's cranky. Maybe we should wait till spring for the next meeting."

Carly got up and headed for her snow boots. "Abby's right. We're fussy, and we can't help it."

Dee Dee crossed her arms and pouted. "Blame it on the weather," she muttered.

"Pout if you want," Carly said. "I'm leaving."

All the kids were staring at her now.

But Carly didn't care. Her stomach did a flitter-flop.

Dee Dee was such a blabbermouth!

FIVE

Carly slid open the skinny door in the closet wall. She flicked on her flashlight.

The guinea pig darted away.

"Sorry about that," Carly said. She shined the light away from his cage. She wanted to keep Piggy company. She wanted to talk to someone. Even a guinea pig was better than Dee Dee Winters!

"The club meeting was horrible tonight. Capital H!" she told Piggy.

The guinea pig rattled his cage.

"Goody, you understand." She reached inside to lift him out. "You're lonely, aren't you?"

Piggy made cute little clicking sounds.

"I'm sorry I had to leave you here." She stroked his soft fur coat.

Piggy seemed to enjoy being petted.

"My best friend blabbed to everyone about your hiding place," she said. "I'll have to keep a close watch on you all weekend. I must take good care of you. Miss Hartman said so."

Piggy seemed to listen. He put his tiny face near her neck.

"Do you have a secret?" Carly leaned her ear down. "Do you know when spring is coming?" she asked. "Like that old groundhog in Pennsylvania?"

She thought of all the icky weather they'd had. One blizzard after another.

Everybody was sick of it. Most of all, Carly!

"Will your cousin see his shadow to-morrow?" she whispered.

Piggy began to whistle loudly.

"Is that an answer?" She had to laugh. "Can you whistle a tune?"

He kept up the shrill sound.

"Let's have a duet." She tried her best to make up a song.

Then . . .

Bam, bam!

Someone was pounding on the sliding door.

She stopped whistling and held her breath. She didn't want to talk to anyone. Especially not big-mouth Dee Dee!

But Piggy kept whistling. Loudly.

"Shh!" she whispered to the guinea pig.

But he continued his Piggy tune.

"I know you're in there, Carly," a voice called through the door.

It was Abby.

Oh no! thought Carly. *She's gonna scold me about the meeting!*

Carly leaned hard against the door.

"Listen," Abby said. "You're not in trouble."

"Go away!" Carly shouted. She felt Piggy tremble in her hand.

"I need to talk to you," Abby insisted.

"What about?"

"About your secret," said Abby.

"What secret?" Carly asked.

"Your idea," Abby said. "Your weather experiment."

Carly did a gulp. "Experiment?" she said. But she knew what Abby meant. Someone had let her secret slip. And she knew who that Someone was.

"Dee Dee told everyone about your plan," Abby said.

I knew it, Carly thought.

"Let me in," Abby called. "Please?"

"Are you mad at me?" Carly asked.

"Why should I be?" Abby said.

Carly waited for her sister to say more. But Abby was quiet.

At last, Carly slid open the door. "I'm sorry about the meeting . . . the way I acted. It wasn't very nice."

Abby smiled. "Don't worry about it," she said. "But tell me about your idea. It sounds *very* exciting. All of us are dying to know if winter is over."

Carly let her big sister into the secret place. Gladly.

They had their own private club meeting. Just two sisters.

And a butterscotch guinea pig.

SIX

Carly slept with Piggy that night. She didn't put the guinea pig under the covers. But she scooted the cage up close to her bed.

"How's that?" she said. "You'll be safe here."

The ball of puff looked sleepy. He'd made a little nest of cedar chips in his cage.

"Ready to dream about springtime?"

Carly hoped so. "Now we'll say our prayers."

Piggy made three clicking sounds. Soft, sleepy ones.

Carly knelt beside her bed. She began to pray. "Dear Lord, please don't let Piggy see his shadow tomorrow. We want some warm weather as soon as possible. It's okay if the Pennsylvania groundhog sees *his* shadow, though. Amen."

She turned out the light and climbed into bed.

"Good night, Piggy," she said. "Sweet dreams of spring."

★ ★ ★

In the middle of the night, Carly opened her eyes. She thought she saw a misty shadow.

She strained her eyes to see. But the bedroom was dark.

"Where's my flashlight?" she mumbled to herself.

Then she remembered. She reached down on the floor and found it. She pointed the light at the shadow.

"Oh no!" she gasped.

It was a Jimmy-shaped shadow!

She sat straight up in bed. "What are you doing?"

"I play with Piggy," Jimmy said. The guinea pig was sitting on his shoulder.

"Better be careful with my pet," she demanded.

"Piggy not just yours." Jimmy had a weird smile. "Piggy belong to all Miss Hartman's class. Jimmy too!"

"But I'm supposed to take care of him." Carly reached for Piggy.

Jimmy backed away. "He like riding here. Piggy like me better than you."

"You're wrong. He'll fall and get hurt," Carly said.

Jimmy began to spin in a circle. Around and around he whirled. He was laughing loudly. He was sure to wake up the whole family!

"Please stop!" Carly said.

But Jimmy kept spinning. And laughing.

Poor Piggy. He was making his dear little whistle sounds. Only now they weren't so little. They were so loud Carly had to cover her ears.

And she was crying. "Please, Jimmy, please . . ."

★   ★   ★

When she opened her eyes, Carly saw her mother.

"Oh . . . where am I?" Carly asked.

"You're right here in your bed,

sweetie," said Mother.

"But Jimmy was twirling Piggy and . . ."

"You were probably dreaming," Mother said. "Jimmy's in his bed sound asleep." She touched Carly's face.

"I thought Piggy might get sick. All that spinning. He could've fallen . . . he could've died."

"Honey, look," Mother said, pointing to the cage. "The guinea pig is perfectly safe."

Carly leaned over her bed to see. Piggy was still curled up in his bed of wood chips. "It *was* a dream. But so real."

Mother was smiling. "Are you ready to go back to sleep?"

"Just a minute." Carly reached down and stroked Piggy's teeny-weeny head. "Now I'm ready."

Her mother tiptoed to the door. "See you in the morning."

"Okay. And no more bad dreams," Carly said.

She really, *really* hoped not.

SEVEN

It was Groundhog Day.

Carly slid Piggy's cage next to her kitchen chair. She sat down for breakfast.

Jimmy slurped his milk across the table. His straight black hair was still damp from his bath. "Why Carly take little pig everywhere?" he asked.

"Because I'm in charge of Piggy," Carly said. "And he isn't a pig."

Jimmy nodded. "I know name of class pet. Miss Hartman tell me, too."

Carly still wanted to protect Piggy. She didn't know what Jimmy might do. Especially after her horrible dream.

Mother brought over a plate of hot waffles. "It's time for the blessing," she said. "Who would like to pray?"

Abby raised her hand. "I'll say grace."

When the prayer was finished, Mother said, "Dee Dee called on the telephone earlier."

Carly perked up her ears. "What did she say?"

"She wants to bring Mister Whiskers over for Groundhog Day." Mother was frowning. "Why does she want to bring her cat here?" she asked.

"Because Carly have secret party," Jimmy said, grinning.

Carly ignored her brother's words. "What did you tell Dee Dee?" Carly asked her mother.

Mother smiled. "I told her to call back after breakfast."

Shawn's eyes lit up. "Can all the cul-de-sac pets come for party?" he asked. "We will see if winter is done."

Carly wasn't so sure. Dee Dee had no right to spoil Carly's experiment. It was *her* idea, after all. A private party for just Piggy and her.

Jimmy asked, too. "Can Jason bring Croaker?" Croaker was the only frog in the cul-de-sac.

Abby poured orange juice in her glass. "It's Carly's party," she said. "She'll decide who comes or not."

Jimmy was whining. "But *I* want to come."

"It's up to Carly to invite you. But only if she wants to."

Carly thought about that. Abby was being kind. She wished Dee Dee wasn't so selfish. It would be lots of fun with all the pets looking for their shadows. That is, *if* the sun was shining.

But Carly hoped the sun wouldn't shine at all. Not today. Then spring would come for sure!

Carly ate her breakfast. But she glanced around the table at her brothers, Shawn and Jimmy. And Abby, too. They looked very eager. Like they couldn't wait for Carly to decide something.

"Mommy make hot cocoa for the party," Jimmy suggested.

Abby's eyes lit up, but she was still.

"We can bake cookies, too," Shawn said. "Serve with hot cocoa at party."

The kids were dying to come to her party. "Okay," she said at last. "Everyone's invited."

"Hoo-ray!" cheered Shawn and Jimmy.

Abby didn't cheer, but she looked happy. Very happy.

Carly felt good all over. "We'll call the experiment a Piggy Party. That stands for the guinea pig, in case you don't get it. Since we don't have a groundhog."

Jimmy spoke in broken English. "We cross fingers for spring. Happy American Groundhog Day."

Carly, Abby, and Shawn clapped their hands.

"Yay!" Carly said. "It's Piggy Party time!"

Abby looked out the window. She groaned. "It's starting to snow again."

Carly was secretly glad. If the sun didn't shine, then Piggy wouldn't see his shadow. Neither would any of the pets.

It was perfect.

Jimmy was shaking his head. "Why Carly make silly weather test?"

"Silly?" Carly pointed at the window. "Look outside. Snow, snow . . . and more snow. Don't you wanna know when this rotten weather's going away?"

Jimmy smiled back. "You very smart sister." It sounded like *velly* smart.

"Thank you," Carly said.

Piggy was rattling his cage. Time to feed him his breakfast of pellets.

"I almost forgot about you," Carly said. She sprinkled some guinea pig food into his little dish.

Shawn came around and peeked into the cage. "Tell Piggy to eat very much breakfast," he said to Carly.

"He's hungry, all right," Carly replied.

They watched the guinea pig eat.

"Piggy need lots of energy," Shawn said. "To hide from shadow."

Carly grinned.

She liked the sound of that!

EIGHT

Carly and Abby swept the snow off their front porch.

"Somebody run and tell Dunkum," Carly said. "We're having the Piggy Party over here."

"We are?" Jason Birchall piped up.

Carly looked over at her sister. "Abby's president. She said so."

Abby stopped sweeping. "It's all right, Jason," she called. "Carly already asked."

Jason stuck his nose in the air. "Carly

already asked," he repeated in a high-pitched voice.

"Okay for you!" Carly grabbed up a mittenful of snow. She threw the snowball at Jason.

Kerplop! It landed on his shoulder.

Eric and Stacy came running across the street. They joined in the snowy fun. Stacy was wearing her new ski outfit.

By the time Dunkum arrived, a snowball fight was in full swing.

"Stop!" Abby shouted. "It's time for the Piggy Party."

Carly threw one more snowball. It landed on Jason's hat.

"Hey! Watch it!" he hollered.

"It was a very soft throw," Carly insisted. She felt someone pulling her away from Jason.

It was Abby. "Come on, you two," said the president of the Cul-de-sac Kids.

Stepping back, Carly lost her balance. *Kerplop!* She fell into a snow pile.

Suddenly, she heard a high whistle.

"Hey! That sounds like Piggy's whistle," she said, looking around.

The kids stopped throwing their snowballs. They tilted their heads, listening.

"Wait a minute," Carly said, worried. "Is the guinea pig outside here somewhere?"

Jimmy spun around in a circle. He was singing a Korean folk song. Faster and faster.

Carly gasped. It was just like her dream. Only Piggy was nowhere to be seen.

She ran to Jimmy. "Where's Piggy?" she asked him.

"Piggy who?" Then Jimmy burst out laughing.

Abby ran to Jimmy. "You *do* know

where he is, don't you?"

"Guess who cannot find his shadow!" Jimmy pulled the guinea pig out of his coat pocket.

There was Piggy. He was snug inside one of Jimmy's socks. The cuff was folded over his neck. It made a big, wide collar around Piggy's tiny neck.

"You could've choked him!" Carly said.

Abby shook her head. "What were you thinking?"

"Jimmy help winter go away. Far away," said Jimmy. He started to cry.

Carly snatched Piggy from Jimmy's hands. "That's no way to help," she said.

She ran into the house. Abby followed her.

"Poor little Piggy," Carly said over and over.

NINE

Carly picked up the telephone. She punched Dee Dee's phone number.

Brring! Brring!

"Hello?" Dee Dee answered.

"Hi, it's Carly calling you back," she said. "You can bring Mister Whiskers to the party."

"I can?"

"Yep." Carly explained that all the kids were invited. "And anyone can bring a pet. Except Jason isn't bringing Croaker."

"Because it's too cold?" Dee Dee said.

"He could freeze his toes off," Carly said.

"What about Piggy?" asked Dee Dee.

"He won't be outside long," said Carly.

She was feeling better toward Dee Dee. Lots better.

Carly glanced at the clock. "It's almost twelve o'clock," she said. "We're having cookies and hot cocoa."

"I'll be right over," Dee Dee said and hung up.

"See ya," said Carly.

★   ★   ★

It was high noon.

On other days, the sun would be shining. Straight up.

Today was different. And Carly was

glad. She crossed her fingers for spring. Capital S!

Gently, she placed Piggy's cage on the snowy ground. Then she got down on her hands and knees. She looked closely.

"How're you doing, little guy?" she whispered.

The guinea pig stuck part of his head through the cage.

"Do you see any shadows anywhere?" she asked.

Piggy twitched his button nose.

No shadow. Not even a teeny-weeny, Piggy-shaped one.

"Yay! Piggy doesn't see his shadow!" she hollered.

The Cul-de-sac Kids cheered.

"Let's take a vote on *all* the pets," Abby called.

"Okay," Carly said. "But it's freezing out here."

"We'll make it quick," Abby promised. She and Shawn gripped their dog Snow White's leash.

"How many pets see their shadows?" Carly asked. She glanced at her best friend. "Start the vote with Dee Dee."

"I vote no. Mister Whiskers can NOT see his shadow," Dee Dee said, cradling her cat. "Too many clouds!"

Eric's hamster was next. "Fran the Ham sees zero shadows," Eric reported. "I vote no."

The kids shouted, "Hoo-ray!"

Stacy Henry was next. "Sunday Funnies, my cockapoo, can't see *his* shadow. I vote no."

"Yay!" the Cul-de-sac Kids cheered.

It was Dunkum's turn. "Mr. Blinkee votes no," said Dunkum, holding his rabbit tight.

"My turn!" hollered Jimmy. He was

leaning over the duck pen near the fence. "Quacker and Jack not see shadows!"

"That's two more NO votes," said Abby.

Jason was doing his usual jig. "Hold everything," he said. "I think . . ." He paused. "Yes, I see my shadow! I really do!"

"What?" Carly said.

"No way!" Abby shouted.

Jason pulled out a flashlight. "See?" He was shining the light on his head.

"Flashlights don't count on Ground-hog Day," Abby scolded.

"Abby's right," Dunkum spoke up.

"Besides, Groundhog Day is just for animals," Carly called.

But Jason was grinning. "Somebody has to be different," he said.

Just then Mister Whiskers got loose.

Meow! Ph-ht! The cat flew across the

snow toward Snow White.

The dog must've seen him coming. She ran across the yard and over the neighbor's fence.

"Somebody do something!" Abby shouted. "Quick!"

Dee Dee ran after her cat. Jason, Jimmy, and Shawn chased after Snow White.

Quacker and Jack flapped their wings. But they bumped against the duck pen.

Fran the Ham spun round and round in his hamster cage.

Blinkee flicked his long ears. He made strange bunny sounds.

Stacy's cockapoo tried to jump out of her arms.

"This is one crazy Piggy Party," Carly muttered. She picked up the guinea pig cage and headed for the house.

It was beginning to snow again. Even harder than before.

Carly dashed to her bedroom. She took Piggy out of his cage and held him close. "I guess winter isn't over yet," she whispered. "But it's not your fault. Not the sun's, either."

TEN

The Cul-de-sac Kids gathered around the kitchen table. The pets had already gone home. Except for Piggy.

"Time for goodies," Carly said.

"Hoo-ray for the treats!" said Jason.

Carly set the guinea pig cage on a chair. "Piggy's the guest of honor," she said.

Jason chuckled. "Some guest."

"Piggy's adorable," Carly said.

"But he didn't see his shadow, did he?" Jason said.

"He couldn't help it if the sun wasn't shining," Carly said.

"It's shining, we just can't see it," Dunkum explained.

"Anybody knows that," Dee Dee said.

"Whatever," Carly said with a grin.

"Okay, kids, listen up," Abby said and unfolded the newspaper. "Has anyone seen the weather page today?"

"I hope it's not bad news," Carly said. She reached for a chocolate chip cookie.

Abby spread the paper out on the table. "We're supposed to have gobs more snow. All week long. The weatherman says so."

Everyone groaned and reached for another cookie.

"Phooey," Carly said. She hated to hear such bad weather news.

Abby folded up the paper. "I guess the seasons have nothing to do with ground-hogs and shadows."

Carly nodded. "Or Piggy Parties."

"Or Cul-de-sac Kids," said Dunkum.

"Not cookies and hot cocoa," said Shawn.

"God is in control of the seasons," Abby replied. "The Bible says so."

Carly couldn't complain. She knew she should've thought of that in the first place!

Click . . . click . . .

Carly glanced at the guinea pig. "Let's hear what Piggy has to say."

The kids stopped sipping hot cocoa.

They stopped chewing their warm cookies.

Click . . . click . . . click . . .

"Does he *really* talk?" asked Eric.

"What's he trying to say?" asked Stacy.

Carly and Dee Dee giggled.

"Oh . . . no, not the giggles," said Jason. He crossed his eyes and covered his ears.

"I think Piggy's trying to tell us he feels left out," Abby said.

Carly stopped giggling. "Hey! Abby's right." And she gave Piggy a snack of pellets.

"He wants to join the Cul-de-sac Kids club," Eric said.

"He's not a kid," said Jason.

"But he's cute," said Stacy.

"He needs a sweater," said Dee Dee.

Carly nodded. "For his trip back to school on Monday."

Jason frowned. "You've got to be kidding. A guinea pig in a sweater?"

Carly couldn't help it. More giggles flew out.

ELEVEN

Time for spelling class.

Click . . . click . . . click . . . Piggy made his soft, happy sounds.

Carly put her pencil down. She stared at the guinea pig across the schoolroom.

I'm glad you came home with me, she thought. *But now you're back at school. Safe and sound.*

"Psst," said Dee Dee behind her. "Miss Hartman is watching you."

Carly picked up her pencil. She wrote

her name at the top of the work sheet. She'd had her fun with the class pet. Now it was time for work.

Miss Hartman would never know what happened. The Piggy Party was Carly's BIG secret. And Jimmy's and Dee Dee's. They'd promised not to tell.

Especially Dee Dee.

★ ★ ★

After spelling came math.

Then it was time for show-and-tell.

One of the boys brought a homemade volcano. He'd made it out of clay, baking soda, and vinegar. The red food coloring made the bubbling soda look like hot lava. *Wow!*

Carly thought it was really neat. She was going to go home and make one, too.

"Who's next for show-and-tell?" asked Miss Hartman.

Dee Dee's hand shot up.

"Yes, Dee Dee?" said Miss Hartman.

Carly wondered what Dee Dee had for show-and-tell. She watched her friend go and stand beside the teacher's desk.

"I don't have anything to show," Dee Dee began.

Some of the classmates snickered.

"But I have something to *tell*." Dee Dee's eyes were shining.

"What is it?" asked Miss Hartman.

Dee Dee's smile was bigger than ever. "I've learned to keep a secret. That's what I have to tell."

Carly's heart sank. She glanced at the guinea pig. What would Dee Dee say?

"I can keep a secret about a Piggy Party," Dee Dee continued. "And about cookies and hot cocoa. About Groundhog Day, too."

Carly scooted down in her seat. Would

Dee Dee tell about the clouds that blocked the sun? Or the guinea pig sweater they'd tried to make?

Quickly, Dee Dee sat down without saying more.

Miss Hartman looked very puzzled. "What's this about a Piggy Party?" asked the teacher. "It sounds very interesting."

"I can't tell. Because it's a secret," said Dee Dee.

Then the boy in front of Carly raised his hand.

"Yes?" said the teacher.

"I have something to show," he said and stood up.

Carly sighed. *Goody,* she thought. *Capital G!*

The Piggy Party secret was safe.

For now.

THE CUL-DE-SAC KIDS SERIES
Don't Miss #20!
THE GRANNY GAME

Abby Hunter's parents are out of town. Grandma Hunter comes to take care of Abby, Carly, Shawn, and Jimmy. And their dog, Snow White, and two ducks, Quacker and Jack.

But soon Granny Mae shows up. She's quite sure that Grandma Hunter needs some help. And the fun begins!

Grandma Hunter is strict and careful. Granny Mae is relaxed and "cool." Will Abby and her siblings survive the wacky weekend? Will they know which Granny to obey?

About the Author

Beverly Lewis thinks guinea pigs are lovable. One summer, she took care of Butterscotch, her niece's pet guinea pig. The furry fellow whistled whenever the refrigerator door opened. (He liked lettuce and other "people food.") Butterscotch also made happy clicking sounds when he was well fed. Just like Piggy!

The show-and-tell volcano (in the last chapter of this book) is especially for Talon Erickson. He knows why.

Be sure to collect ALL the Cul-de-sac Kids books in the series. You'll whistle your way to adventure and mystery. And fun, fun, fun!

Also by Beverly Lewis

GIRLS ONLY (GO!)
Youth Fiction

Dreams on Ice   *Only the Best*

SUMMERHILL SECRETS
Youth Fiction

Whispers Down the Lane   *A Cry in the Dark*
Secret in the Willows   *House of Secrets*
Catch a Falling Star   *Echoes in the Wind*
Night of the Fireflies   *Hide Behind the Moon*
Windows on the Hill

HOLLY'S HEART SERIES
Youth Fiction

Holly's First Love   *Straight-A Teacher*
Secret Summer Dreams   *The "No-Guys" Pact*
Sealed With a Kiss   *Little White Lies*
The Trouble With Weddings   *Freshmen Frenzy*
California Christmas   *Mystery Letters*
Second-Best Friend   *Eight Is Enough*
Good-bye, Dressel Hills   *It's a Girl Thing*

THE HERITAGE OF LANCASTER COUNTY
Adult Fiction

The Shunning   *The Confession*
The Reckoning

GIFT BOOK

The Sunroom

Series for Young Readers*
From Bethany House Publishers

★ ★ ★

THE ADVENTURES OF CALLIE ANN
by Shannon Mason Leppard

Readers will giggle their way through the true-to-life escapades of Callie Ann Davies and her many North Carolina friends.

★ ★ ★

BACKPACK MYSTERIES
by Mary Carpenter Reid

This excitement-filled mystery series follows the mishaps and adventures of Steff and Paulie Larson as they strive to help often-eccentric relatives crack their toughest cases.

★ ★ ★

THE CUL-DE-SAC KIDS
by Beverly Lewis

Each story in this lighthearted series features the hilarious antics and predicaments of nine endearing boys and girls who live on Blossom Hill Lane.

★ ★ ★

RUBY SLIPPERS SCHOOL
by Stacy Towle Morgan

Join the fun as home-schoolers Hope and Annie Brown visit fascinating countries and meet inspiring Christians from around the world!

★ ★ ★

THREE COUSINS DETECTIVE CLUB®
by Elspeth Campbell Murphy

Famous detective cousins Timothy, Titus, and Sarah-Jane learn compelling Scripture-based truths while finding—and solving—intriguing mysteries.

* (ages 7–10)